Evergreens

By

Jerome K. Jerome

British Library Cataloguing-in-Publication Data
A catalogue record for this book is available from the
British Library

Jerome K. Jerome

Jerome Klapka Jerome was born in Walsall, England in 1859. Both his parents died while he was in his early teens, and he was forced to quit school to support himself. Jerome worked for a number of years collecting coal along railway tracks, before trying his hand at acting, journalism, teaching and soliciting. At long last, in 1885, he had some success with *On the Stage – and Off,* a comic memoir of his experiences with an acting troupe. Jerome produced a number of essays over the following years, and married in 1888, spending the honeymoon in "a little boat" on the Thames.

In 1889, Jerome published his most successful and best-remembered work, *Three Men in a Boat.* Featuring himself and two of his friends encountering humorous situations while floating down the Thames in a small boat, the book was an instant success, and has never been out of print. In fact, its popularity was such that the number of registered Thames boats went up fifty percent in the year following its publication. With the financial security provided by *Three Men in a Boat,* Jerome was able to dedicate himself fully to writing, producing eleven more novels and a number of anthologies of short fiction.

In 1926, Jerome published his autobiography, *My Life and Times.* He died a year later, aged 68.

They look so dull and dowdy in the spring weather, when the snow drops and the crocuses are putting on their dainty frocks of white and mauve and yellow, and the baby-buds from every branch are peeping with bright eyes out on the world, and stretching forth soft little leaves toward the coming gladness of their lives. They stand apart, so cold and hard amid the stirring hope and joy that are throbbing all around them.

And in the deep full summer-time, when all the rest of nature dons its richest garb of green, and the roses clamber round the porch, and the grass waves waist-high in the meadow, and the fields are gay with flowers—they seem duller and dowdier than ever then, wearing their faded winter's dress, looking so dingy and old and worn.

In the mellow days of autumn, when the trees, like dames no longer young, seek to forget their aged looks under gorgeous bright-toned robes of gold and brown and purple, and the grain is yellow in the fields, and the ruddy fruit hangs clustering from the drooping boughs, and the wooded hills in their thousand hues stretched like leafy rainbows above the vale—ah! surely they look their dullest and dowdiest then. The gathered glory of the dying year is all around them. They seem so out of place among it, in their somber, everlasting green, like poor relations at a rich man's feast. It is such a weather-beaten old green dress. So many summers' suns have blistered it, so many winters' rains have beat upon it—

such a shabby, mean, old dress; it is the only one they have!

They do not look quite so bad when the weary winter weather is come, when the flowers are dead, and the hedgerows are bare, and the trees stand out leafless against the gray sky, and the birds are all silent, and the fields are brown, and the vine clings round the cottages with skinny, fleshless arms, and they alone of all things are unchanged, they alone of all the forest are green, they alone of all the verdant host stand firm to front the cruel winter.

They are not very beautiful, only strong and stanch and steadfast—the same in all times, through all seasons—ever the same, ever green. The spring cannot brighten them, the summer cannot scorch them, the autumn cannot wither them, the winter cannot kill them.

There are evergreen men and women in the world, praise be to God! Not many of them, but a few. They are not the showy folk; they are not the clever, attractive folk. (Nature is an old-fashioned shopkeeper; she never puts her best goods in the window.) They are only the quiet, strong folk; they are stronger than the world, stronger than life or death, stronger than Fate. The storms of life sweep over them, and the rains beat down upon them, and the biting frosts creep round them; but the winds and the rains and the frosts pass away, and they are still standing, green and straight. They love the sunshine of life in their undemonstrative way—its pleasures, its joys. But calamity cannot bow them, sorrow and affliction bring not despair to their serene faces, only a little tightening of the lips; the sun of our prosperity makes the green of their friendship no brighter, the frost of our adversity kills not the leaves of their affection.

Let us lay hold of such men and women; let us grapple them to us with hooks of steel; let us cling to them as we would to rocks in a tossing sea. We do not think very much of them in the summertime of life. They do not flatter us or gush over us. They do not always agree with us. They are not always the most delightful society, by any means. They are not good talkers, nor—which would do just as well, perhaps better—do they make enraptured listeners. They have awkward manners, and very little tact. They do not shine to advantage beside our society friends. They do not dress well; they look altogether somewhat dowdy and commonplace. We almost hope they will not see us when we meet them just outside the club. They are not the sort of people we want to ostentatiously greet in crowded places. It is not till the days of our need that we learn to love and know them. It is not till the winter that the birds see the wisdom of building their nests in the evergreen trees.

And we, in our spring-time folly of youth, pass them by with a sneer, the uninteresting, colorless evergreens, and, like silly children with nothing but eyes in their heads, stretch out our hands and cry for the pretty flowers. We will make our little garden of life such a charming, fairy-like spot, the envy of every passer-by! There shall nothing grow in it but lilies and roses, and the cottage we will cover all over with Virginia-creeper. And, oh, how sweet it will look, under the dancing summer sun-light, when the soft west breeze is blowing!

And, oh, how we shall stand and shiver there when the rain and the east wind come!

Oh, you foolish, foolish little maidens, with your dainty heads so full of unwisdom! how often—oh! how often, are you to be warned that it is not always the sweetest thing in lovers that is the best material to make a good-wearing husband out of? "The lover sighing like a furnace" will not go on sighing like a furnace forever. That furnace will go out. He will become the husband, "full of strange oaths—jealous in honor, sudden and quick in quarrel," and grow "into the lean and slipper'd pantaloon." How will he wear? There will be no changing him if he does not suit, no sending him back to be altered, no having him let out a bit where he is too tight and hurts you, no having him taken in where he is too loose, no laying him by when the cold comes, to wrap yourself up in something warmer. As he is when you select him, so he will have to last you all your life—through all changes, through all seasons.

Yes, he looks very pretty now—handsome pattern, if the colors are fast and it does not fade—feels soft and warm to the touch. How will he stand the world's rough weather? How will he stand life's wear and tear?

He looks so manly and brave. His hair curls so divinely. He dresses so well (I wonder if the tailor's bill is paid?) He kisses your hand so gracefully. He calls you such pretty names. His arm feels so strong a round you. His fine eyes are so full of tenderness as they gaze down into yours.

Will he kiss your hand when it is wrinkled and old? Will he call you pretty names when the baby is crying in the night, and you cannot keep it quiet—or, better still, will he sit up and take a turn with it? Will his arm be strong around you in the days of trouble? Will his eyes shine above you full of tenderness when yours are growing dim?

And you boys, you silly boys! what materials for a wife do you think you will get out of the empty-headed coquettes you are raving and tearing your hair about. Oh! yes, she is very handsome, and she dresses with exquisite taste (the result of devoting the whole of her heart, mind and soul to the subject, and never allowing her thoughts to be distracted from it by any other mundane or celestial object whatsoever); and she is very agreeable and entertaining and fascinating; and she will go on looking handsome, and dressing exquisitely, and being agreeable and entertaining and fascinating just as much after you have married her as before—more so, if anything.

But *you* will not get the benefit of it. Husbands will be charmed and fascinated by her in plenty, but *you* will not be among them. You will run the show, you will pay all the expenses, do all the work. Your performing lady will be most affable and enchanting to the crowd. They will stare at her, and admire her, and talk to her, and flirt with her. And you will be able to feel that you are quite a benefactor to your fellow-men and women—to your fellow-men especially—in providing such delightful amusement for them, free. But *you* will not get any of the fun yourself.

You will not get the handsome looks. *You* will get the jaded face, and the dull, lusterless eyes, and the untidy hair with the dye showing on it. You will not get the exquisite dresses. *You* will get dirty, shabby frocks and slommicking dressing-gowns, such as your cook would be ashamed to wear. *You* will not get the charm and fascination. *You* will get the after-headaches, the complainings and grumblings, the silence and sulkiness, the weariness and lassitude and ill-temper that comes as such a relief after working hard all day at being pleasant!

It is not the people who shine in society, but the people who brighten up the back parlor; not the people who are charming when they are out, but the people who are charming when they are in, that are good to *live* with. It is not the brilliant men and women, but the simple, strong, restful men and women, that make the best traveling companions for the road of life. The men and women who will only laugh as they put up the umbrella when the rain begins to fall, who will trudge along cheerfully through the mud and over the stony places—the comrades who will lay their firm hand on ours and strengthen us when the way is dark and we are growing weak—the evergreen men and women, who, like the holly, are at their brightest and best when the blast blows chilliest—the stanch men and women!

It is a grand thing this stanchness. It is the difference between a dog and a sheep—between a man and an oyster.

Women, as a rule, are stancher than men. There are women that you feel you could rely upon to the death. But very few men indeed have this dog-like virtue. Men, taking them generally, are more like cats. You may live with them and call them yours for twenty years, but you can never feel *quite* sure of them. You never know exactly what they are thinking of. You never feel easy in your mind as to the result of the next-door neighbor's laying down a Brussels carpet in his kitchen.

We have no school for the turning-out of stanch men in this nineteenth century. In the old, earnest times, war made men stanch and true to each other. We have learned up a good many glib phrases about the wickedness of war, and we thank God that we live in these peaceful, trading times, wherein we can—and do—devote the whole our thoughts and energies to robbing and cheating and swindling one another—to "doing" our friends, and overcoming our enemies by trickery and lies—wherein, undisturbed by the wicked ways of fighting-men, we can cultivate to better perfection the "smartness," the craft, and the cunning, and all the other "business-like" virtues on which we so pride ourselves, and which were so neglected and treated with so little respect in the bad old age of violence, when men chose lions and eagles for their symbols rather than foxes.

There is a good deal to be said against war. I am not prepared to maintain that war did not bring with it disadvantages, but there can be no doubt that, for the noblest work of Nature—the making of men—it was a splendid manufactory. It taught men courage. It trained them in promptness and determination, in strength of brain and strength of hand. From its stern lessons they learned fortitude in suffering, coolness in danger, cheerfulness under reverses. Chivalry, Reverence, and Loyalty are the beautiful children of ugly War. But, above all gifts, the greatest gift it gave to men was stanchness.

It first taught men to be true to one another; to be true to their duty, true to their post; to be in all things faithful, even unto death.

The martyrs that died at the stake; the explorers that fought with Nature and opened up the world for us; the reformers (they had to do something more than talk in those days) who won for us our liberties; the men who gave their lives to science and art, when science and art brought, not as now, fame and fortune, but shame and penury—they sprang from the loins of the rugged men who had learned, on many a grim battlefield, to laugh at pain and death, who had had it hammered into them, with many a hard blow, that the whole duty of a man in this world is to be true to his trust, and fear not.

Do you remember the story of the old Viking who had been converted to Christianity, and who, just as they were about, with much joy, to baptize him, paused and asked: "But what—if this, as you tell me, is the only way to the true Valhalla—what has become of my comrades, my friends who are dead, who died in the old faith—where are they?"

The priests, confused, replied there could be no doubt those unfortunate folk had gone to a place they would rather not mention.

"Then," said the old warrior, stepping back, "I will not be baptized. I will go along with my own people."

He had lived with them, fought beside them; they were his people. He would stand by them to the end—of eternity. Most assuredly, a very shocking old Viking! But I think it might be worth while giving up our civilization and our culture to get back to the days when they made men like that.

The only reminder of such times that we have left us now, is the bull-dog; and he is fast dying out—the pity of it! What a splendid old dog he is! so grim, so silent, so stanch; so terrible, when he has got his idea, of his duty clear before him; so absurdly meek, when it is only himself that is concerned.

He is the gentlest, too, and the most lovable of all dogs. He does not look it. The sweetness of his disposition would not strike the casual observer at first glance. He resembles the gentleman spoken of in the oft-quoted stanza:

> 'E's all right when yer knows 'im.
> But yer've got to know 'im fust.

The first time I ever met a bull-dog—to speak to, that is—was many years ago. We were lodging down in the country, an orphan friend of mine named George, and myself, and one night, coming home late from some dissolving views we found the family had gone to bed. They had left a light in our room, however, and we went in and sat down, and began to take off our boots.

And then, for the first time, we noticed on the hearthrug a bull-dog. A dog with a more thoughtfully ferocious expression—a dog with, apparently, a heart more dead to all ennobling and civilizing sentiments—I have never seen. As George said, he looked more like some heathen idol than a happy English dog.

He appeared to have been waiting for us; and he rose up and greeted us with a ghastly grin, and got between us and the door.

We smiled at him—a sickly, propitiatory smile. We said, "Good dog—poor fellow!" and we asked him, in tones implying that the question could admit of no negative, if he was not a "nice old chap." We did not really think so. We had our own private opinion concerning him, and it was unfavorable. But we did not express it. We would not have hurt his feelings for the world. He was a visitor, our guest, so to speak—and, as well-brought-up young men, we felt that the right thing to do was for us to prevent his gaining any hint that we were not glad to see him, and to make him feel as little as possible the awkwardness of his position.

I think we succeeded. He was singularly unembarrassed, and far more at his ease than even we were. He took but little notice of our flattering remarks, but was much drawn toward George's legs. George used to be, I remember, rather proud of his legs. I could never see enough in them myself to excuse George's vanity; indeed, they always struck me as lumpy. It is only fair to acknowledge, however, that they quite fascinated that bull-dog. He walked over and criticized them with the air of a long-baffled connoisseur who had at last found his ideal. At the termination of his inspection he distinctly smiled.

George, who at that time was modest and bashful, blushed and drew them up on to the chair. On the dog's displaying a desire to follow them, George moved up on to the table, and squatted there in the middle, nursing his knees. George's legs being lost to him, the dog appeared inclined to console himself with mine. I went and sat beside George on the table.

Sitting with your feet drawn up in front of you, on a small and rickety one-legged table, is a most trying exercise, especially if you are not used to it. George and I both felt our position keenly. We did not like to call out for help, and bring the family down. We were proud young men, and we feared lest, to the unsympathetic eye of the comparative stranger, the spectacle we should present might not prove imposing.

We sat on in silence for about half an hour, the dog keeping a reproachful eye upon us from the nearest chair, and displaying elephantine delight whenever we made any movement suggestive of climbing down.

At the end of the half hour we discussed the advisability of "chancing it," but decided not to. "We should never," George said, "confound foolhardiness with courage."

"Courage," he continued—George had quite a gift for maxims—"courage is the wisdom of manhood; foolhardiness, the folly of youth."

He said that to get down from the table while that dog remained in the room, would clearly prove us to be possessed of the latter quality; so we restrained ourselves, and sat on.

We sat on for over an hour, by which time, having both grown careless of life and indifferent to the voice of Wisdom, we did "chance it;" and throwing the table-cloth over our would-be murderer, charged for the door and got out.

The next morning we complained to our landlady of her carelessness in leaving wild beasts about the place, and we gave her a brief if not exactly truthful, history of the business.

Instead of the tender womanly sympathy we had expected, the old lady sat down in the easy chair and burst out laughing.

"What! old Boozer," she exclaimed, "you was afraid of old Boozer! Why, bless you, he wouldn't hurt a worm! He ain't got a tooth in his head, he ain't; we has to feed him with a spoon; and I'm sure the way the cat chivies him about must be enough to make his life a burden to him. I expect he wanted you to nurse him; he's used to being nursed."

And that was the brute that had kept us sitting on a table, with our boots off, for over an hour on a chilly night!

Another bull-dog exhibition that occurs to me was one given by my uncle. He had had a bulldog—a young one—given to him by a friend. It was a grand dog, so his friend had told him; all it wanted was training—it had not been properly trained. My uncle did not profess to know much about the training of bull-dogs; but it seemed a simple enough matter, so he thanked the man, and took his prize home at the end of a rope.

"Have we got to live in the house with *this?*" asked my aunt, indignantly, coming in to the room about an hour after the dog's advent, followed by the quadruped himself, wearing an idiotically self-satisfied air.

"That!" exclaimed my uncle, in astonishment; "why, it's a splendid dog. His father was honorably mentioned only last year at the Aquarium."

"Ah, well, all I can say is, that his son isn't going the way to get honorably mentioned in this neighborhood," replied my aunt, with bitterness; "he's just finished killing poor Mrs. McSlanger's cat, if you want to know what he has been doing. And a pretty row there'll be about it, too!"

"Can't we hush it up?" said my uncle.

"Hush it up?" retorted my aunt. "If you'd heard the row, you wouldn't sit there and talk like a fool. And if you'll take my advice," added my aunt, "you'll set to work on this 'training,' or whatever it is, that has got to be done to the dog, before any human life is lost."

My uncle was too busy to devote any time to the dog for the next day or so, and all that could be done was to keep the animal carefully confined to the house.

And a nice time we had with him! It was not that the animal was bad-hearted. He meant well—he tried to do his duty. What was wrong with him was that he was too hard-working. He wanted to do too much. He started with an exaggerated and totally erroneous notion of his duties and responsibilities. His idea was that he had been brought into the house for the purpose of preventing any living human soul from coming near it and of preventing any person who might by chance have managed to slip in from ever again leaving it.

We endeavored to induce him to take a less exalted view of his position, but in vain. That was the conception he had formed in his own mind concerning his earthly task, and that conception he insisted on living up to with, what appeared to us to be, unnecessary conscientiousness.

He so effectually frightened away all the trades people, that they at last refused to enter the gate. All that they would do was to bring their goods and drop them over the fence into the front garden, from where we had to go and fetch them as we wanted them.

"I wish you'd run into the garden," my aunt would say to me—I was stopping with them at the time—"and see if you can find any sugar; I think there's some under the big rose-bush. If not, you'd better go to Jones' and order some."

And on the cook's inquiring what she should get ready for lunch, my aunt would say:

"Well, I'm sure, Jane, I hardly know. What have we? Are there any chops in the garden, or was it a bit of steak that I noticed on the lawn?"

On the second afternoon the plumbers came to do a little job to the kitchen boiler. The dog, being engaged at the time in the front of the house, driving away the postman, did not notice their arrival. He was broken-hearted at finding them there when he got downstairs, and evidently blamed himself most bitterly. Still, there they were, all owing to his carelessness, and the only thing to be done now was to see that they did not escape.

There were three plumbers (it always takes three plumbers to do a job; the first man comes on ahead to tell you that the second man will be there soon, the second man comes to say that he can't stop, and the third man follows to ask if the first man has been there); and that faithful, dumb animal kept them pinned up in the kitchen—fancy wanting to keep plumbers in a house longer than is absolutely necessary!—for five hours, until my uncle came home; and the bill ran: "Self and two men engaged six hours, repairing boiler-tap, 18s.; material, 2d.; total 18s. 2d."

He took a dislike to the cook from the very first. We did not blame him for this. She was a disagreeable old woman, and we did not think much of her ourselves. But when it came to keeping her out of the kitchen, so that she could not do her work, and my aunt and uncle had to cook the dinner themselves, assisted by the housemaid—a willing-enough girl, but necessarily inexperienced—we felt that the woman was being subject to persecution.

My uncle, after this, decided that the dog's training must be no longer neglected. The man next door but one always talked as if he knew a lot about sporting matters, and to him my uncle went for advice as to how to set about it.

"Oh, yes," said the man, cheerfully, "very simple thing, training a bull-dog. Wants patience, that's all."

"Oh, that will be all right," said my uncle; "it can't want much more than living in the same house with him before he's trained does. How do you start?"

"Well, I'll tell you," said next-door-but-one. "You take him up into a room where there's not much furniture, and you shut the door and bolt it."

"I see," said my uncle.

"Then you place him on the floor in the middle of the room, and you go down on your knees in front of him, and begin to irritate him."

"Oh!"

"Yes—and you go on irritating him until you have made him quite savage."

"Which, from what I know of the dog, won't take long," observed my uncle thoughtfully.

"So much the better. The moment he gets savage he will fly at you."

My uncle agreed that the idea seemed plausible.

"He will fly at your throat," continued the next-door-but-one man, "and this is where you will have to be careful. *As* he springs toward you, and *before* he gets hold of you, you must hit him a fair straight blow on his nose, and knock him down."

"Yes, I see what you mean."

"Quite so—well, the moment you have knocked him down, he will jump up and go for you again. You must knock him down again; and you must keep on doing this, until the dog is thoroughly cowed and exhausted. Once he is thoroughly cowed, the thing's done—dog's as gentle as a lamb after that."

"Oh!" says my uncle, rising from his chair, "you think that a good way, do you?"

"Certainly," replied the next-door-but-one man; "it never fails."

"Oh! I wasn't doubting it," said my uncle; "only it's just occurred to me that as you understand the knack of these things, perhaps *you'd* like to come in and try *your* hand on the dog? We can give you a room quite to yourselves; and I'll undertake that nobody comes near to interfere with you. And if—if," continued my uncle, with that kindly thoughtfulness which ever distinguished his treatment of others, "*if*, by any chance, you should miss hitting the dog at the proper critical moment, or, if *you* should get cowed and exhausted first, instead of the dog—why, I shall only be too pleased to take the whole burden of the funeral expenses on my own shoulders; and I hope you know me well enough to feel sure that the arrangements will be tasteful, and, at the same time, unostentatious!"

And out my uncle walked.

We next consulted the butcher, who agreed that the prize-ring method was absurd, especially when recommended to a short-winded, elderly family man, and who recommended, instead, plenty of out-door exercise for the dog, under my uncle's strict supervision and control.

"Get a fairly long chain for him," said the butcher, "and take him out for a good stiff run every evening. Never let him get away from you; make him mind you, and bring him home always thoroughly exhausted. You stick to that for a month or two, regular, and you'll have him like a little child."

"Um!—seems to me that I'm going to get more training over his job than anybody else," muttered my uncle, as he thanked the man and left the shop; "but I suppose it's got to be done. Wish I'd never had the d— dog now!"

So, religiously, every evening, my uncle would fasten a long chain to that poor dog, and drag him away from his happy home with the idea of exhausting him; and the dog would come back as fresh as paint, my uncle behind him, panting and clamoring for brandy.

My uncle said he should never have dreamed there could have been such stirring times in this prosaic nineteenth century as he had, training that dog.

Oh, the wild, wild scamperings over the breezy common—the dog trying to catch a swallow, and my uncle, unable to hold him back, following at the other end of the chain!

Oh, the merry frolics in the fields, when the dog wanted to kill a cow, and the cow wanted to kill the dog, and they each dodged round my uncle, trying to do it!

And, oh, the pleasant chats with the old ladies when the dog wound the chain into a knot around their legs, and upset them, and my uncle had to sit down in the road beside them, and untie them before they could get up again!

But a crisis came at last. It was a Saturday afternoon—uncle being exercised by dog in usual way—nervous children playing in road, see dog, scream, and run—playful young dog thinks it a game, jerks chain out of uncle's grasp, and flies after them—uncle flies after dog, calling it names—fond parent in front garden, seeing beloved children chased by savage dog, followed by careless owner, flies after uncle, calling *him* names—householders come to doors and cry, "Shame!"—also throw things at dog—things don't hit dog, hit uncle—things that don't hit uncle, hit fond parent—through the village and up the hill, over the bridge and round by the green—grand run, mile and a half without a break! Children sink exhausted—dog gambols up among them—children go into fits—fond parent and uncle come up together, both breathless.

"Why don't you call your dog off, you wicked old man?"

"Because I can't recollect his name, you old fool, you!"

Fond parent accuses uncle of having set dog on—uncle, indignant, reviles fond parent—exasperated fond parent attacks uncle—uncle retaliates with umbrella—faithful dog comes to assistance of uncle, and inflicts great injury on fond parent—arrival of police—dog attacks police—uncle and fond parent both taken into custody—uncle fined five pounds and costs for keeping a ferocious dog at large—uncle fined five pounds and costs for assault on fond parent—uncle fined five pounds and cost for assault on police!

My uncle gave the dog away soon after that. He did not waste him. He gave him as a wedding-present to a near relation.

But the saddest story I ever heard in connection with a bull-dog, was one told by my aunt herself.

Now you can rely upon this story, because it is not one of mine, it is one of my aunt's, and she would scorn to tell a lie. This is a story you could tell to the heathen, and feel that you were teaching them the truth and doing them good. They give this story out at all the Sunday-schools in our part of the country, and draw moral lessons from it. It is a story that a little child can believe.

It happened in the old crinoline days. My aunt, who was then living in a country-town, had gone out shopping one morning, and was standing in the High Street, talking to a lady friend, a Mrs. Gumworthy, the doctor's wife. She (my aunt) had on a new crinoline that morning, in which, to use her own expression, she rather fancied herself. It was a tremendously big one, as stiff as a wire-fence; and it "set" beautifully.

They were standing in front of Jenkins', the draper's; and my aunt thinks that it—the crinoline—must have got caught up in something, and an opening thus left between it and the ground. However this may be, certain it is that an absurdly large and powerful bull-dog, who was fooling round about there at the time, managed, somehow or other, to squirm in under my aunt's crinoline, and effectually imprison himself beneath it.

Finding himself suddenly in a dark and gloomy chamber, the dog, naturally enough, got frightened, and made frantic rushes to get out. But whichever way he charged; there was the crinoline in front of him. As he flew, he, of course, carried it before him, and with the crinoline, of course, went my aunt.

But nobody knew the explanation. My aunt herself did not know what had happened. Nobody had seen the dog creep inside the crinoline. All that the people did see was a staid and eminently respectable middle-aged lady suddenly, and without any apparent reason, throw her umbrella down in the road, fly up the High Street at the rate of ten miles an hour, rush across it at the imminent risk of her life, dart down it again on the other side, rush sideways, like an excited crab, into a grocer's shop, run three times round the shop, upsetting the whole stock-in-trade, come out of the shop backward and knock down a postman, dash into the roadway and spin round twice, hover for a moment, undecided, on the curb, and then away up the hill again, as if she had only just started, all the while screaming out at the top of her voice for somebody to stop her!

Of course, everybody thought she was mad. The people flew before her like chaff before the wind. In less than five seconds the High Street was a desert. The townsfolk scampered into their shops and houses and barricaded the doors. Brave men dashed out and caught up little children and bore them to places of safety amid cheers. Carts and carriages were abandoned, while the drivers climbed up lamp-posts!

What would have happened had the affair gone on much longer—whether my aunt would have been shot, or the fire-engine brought into requisition against her— it is impossible, having regard to the terrified state of the crowd, to say. Fortunately for her, she became exhausted. With one despairing shriek she gave way, and sat down on the dog; and peace reigned once again in that sweet rural town.

THE END.